For William

First published in hardback in Great Britain by HarperCollins Publishers Ltd in 1996
First published in Picture Lions in 1997
5 7 9 10 8 6 4
ISBN: 0 00 664593 3
Picture Lions is an imprint of the Children's Division, part of HarperCollins Publishers Ltd, 77-85 Fulham
Palace Road, Hammersmith, London W6 8JB.
Text and illustrations copyright © John Wallace 1996
The author/illustrator asserts the moral right to be identified as the author/illustrator of the work.
A CIP catalogue for this title is available from the British Library.
Printed and bound in Hong Kong.

Little Bean's Friend

John Wallace

PictureLions

An Imprint of HarperCollins*Publishers*

Little Bean!

You're making far too much noise.

Right! That is it!

Outside the pair of you!

Go on, it's a lovely day!

Little Bean put on her swimsuit
and ran outside. There was the
whole garden to play in.

Little Bean went
on her slide,

and played in the
Wendy house.

She played in
the sand pit,

and with the
hose pipe.

She rode on
her tricycle,

and splashed in
the paddling pool.

Then when the sun went in
Little Bean got changed,

and ran
outside again,

and played chase until…

she got too excited and lost her
favourite teddy.

There was no way of getting it back.

"Is this yours?"

Little Bean ran inside,

and told her Daddy.

"It's only that nice Paul next door."

"Why don't you pop over and say hello?"

"Hello, Nice Paul. I'm Little Bean."

They played together
on the slide,

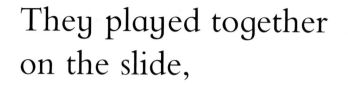

and in the
Wendy house.

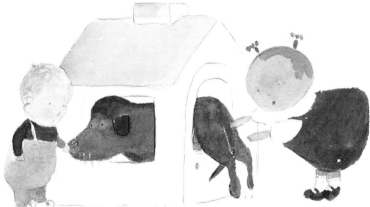

They played
in the sand pit,

and with the hose pipe.

They played with the tricycle,

and splashed in
the paddling pool.

"Will you be my friend tomorrow?"